first book my first book my first
k my first book my first book my
ook my first book my first book
first book my first book my first
k my first book my first book my
ook my first book my first book
first book my first book my first
k my first book my first book my
ook my first book my first book
first book my first book my first
k my first book my first book my
ook my first book my first book
first book my first book my first

my first book my first book my f
book my first book my first boo
my first book my first book my f
book my first book my first bool
my first book my first book my f
book my first book my first bool
my first book my first book my f
book my first book my first bool
my first book my first book my f
book my first book my first bool
my first book my first book my f
book my first book my first bool
my first book my first book my f

My First Book

Library of Congress Cataloging-in-Publication Data
Moncure, Jane Belk.
My first book / by Jane Belk Moncure; illustrated by Colin King.
p. cm.
Summary: Each illustration is accompanied by a single word that identifies it.
ISBN 1-56766-765-1 (lib. bdg. : alk. paper)
[1. Vocabulary.] I. King, Colin, ill. II. Title.
PZ7.M739 Myfi 2000
[E]—dc21   99-055406

My First Book

Jane Belk Moncure

illustrated by Colin King

The Child's World®

eyes

nose

mouth

hair

feet

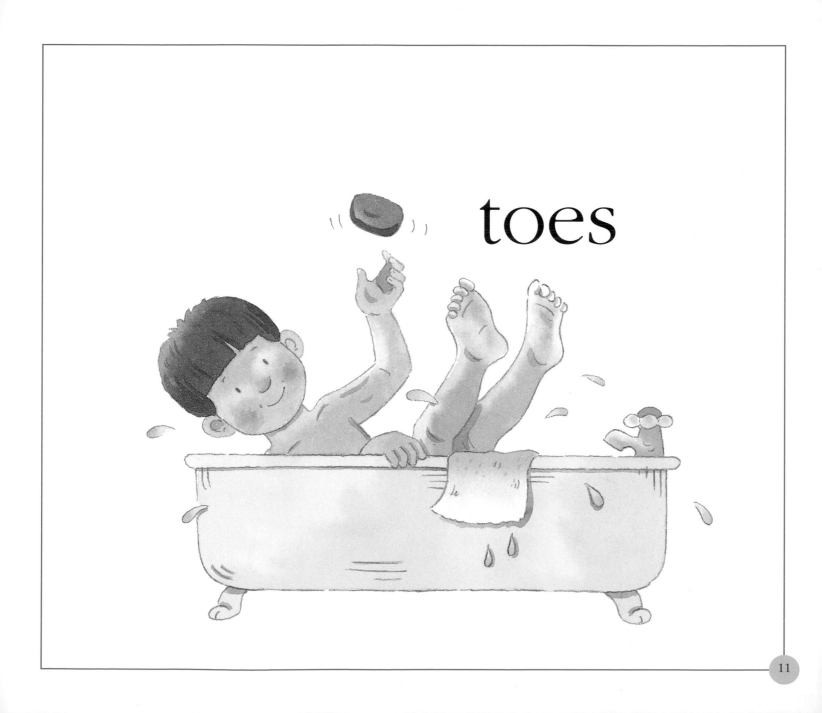

toes

Mommy

Daddy

hug

friends

balloons

hats

pajamas

bed

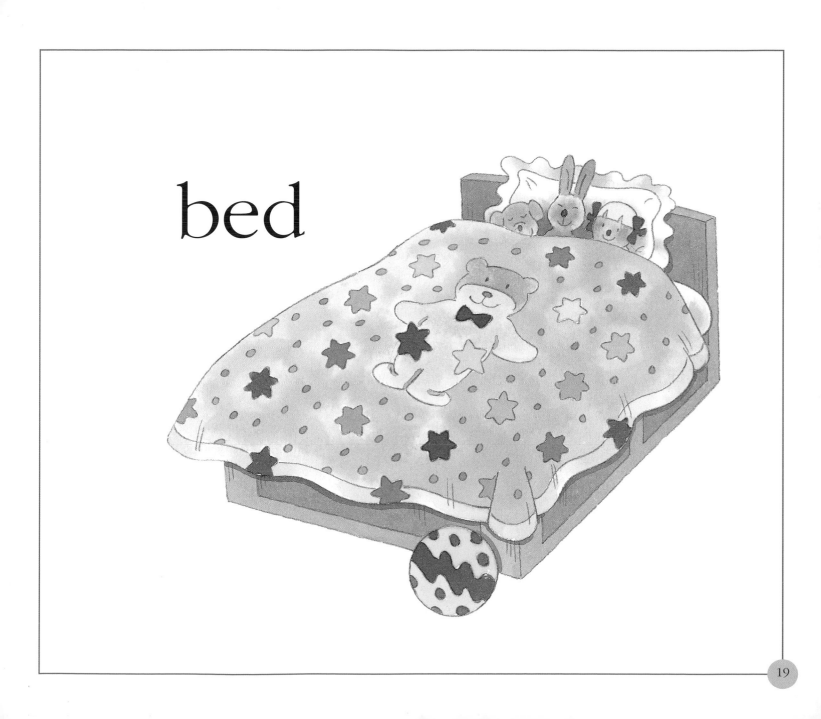

cup

plate

apple

cookies

ball

wagon

bear

doll

bunny

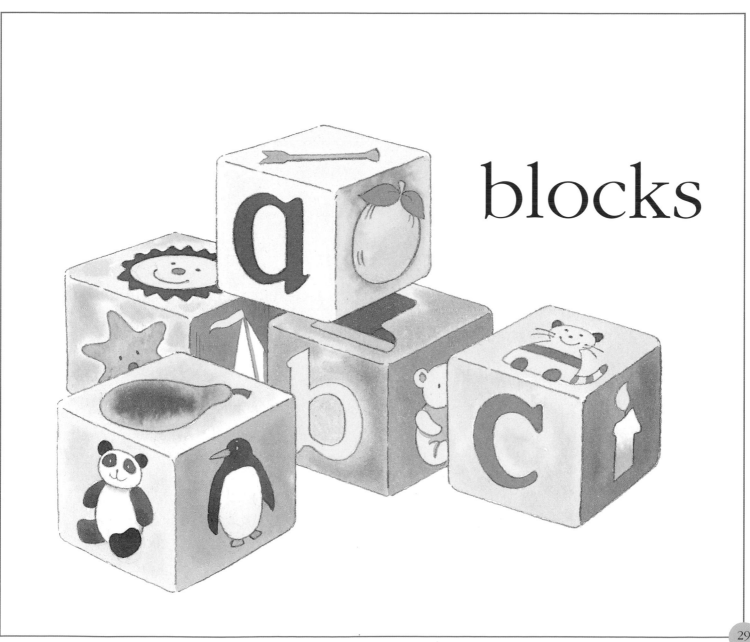

blocks

box

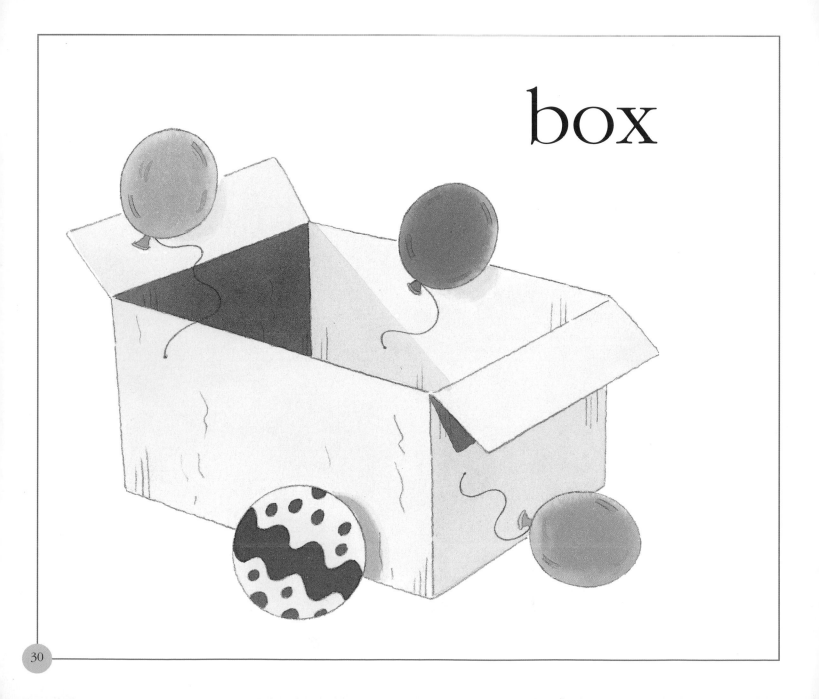

I will fill my box.

ABOUT THE AUTHOR AND ILLUSTRATOR

Jane Belk Moncure began her writing career when she was in kindergarten. She has never stopped writing. Many of her children's stories and poems have been published, to the delight of young readers, including her son Jim, whose childhood experiences found their way into many of her books.

Mrs. Moncure's writing is based upon an active career in early childhood education.
A recipient of an M.A. degree from Columbia University, Mrs. Moncure has taught and directed nursery, kindergarten, and primary grade programs in California, New York, Virginia, and North Carolina. As a former member of the faculties of Virginia Commonwealth University and the University of Richmond, she taught prospective teachers in early childhood education.

Mrs. Moncure has travelled extensively abroad, studying early childhood programs in the United Kingdom, The Netherlands, and Switzerland. She was the first president of the Virginia Association for Early Childhood Education and received its award for outstanding service to young children.

A resident of North Carolina, Mrs. Moncure is currently a full-time writer and educational consultant. She is married to Dr. James A. Moncure, former vice president of Elon College.

Colin King studied at the Royal College of Art, London. He started his freelance career as an illustrator, working for magazines and advertising agencies.

He began drawing pictures for children's books in 1976 and has illustrated over sixty titles to date.

Included in a wide variety of subjects are a best-selling children's encyclopedia and books about spies and detectives.

His books have been translated into several languages, including Japanese and Hebrew. He has four grown-up children and lives in Suffolk, England, with his wife, three dogs, and a cat.